THE SESAME STREET
TREASURY

Featuring Jim Henson's Sesame Street Muppets

VOLUME 2

STARRING
THE NUMBER
2
AND THE LETTER
B

Children's Television Workshop/Funk & Wagnalls, Inc.

WRITTEN BY:

Linda Bove with
the National Theatre of the Deaf
Michael Frith
Emily Perl Kingsley
Sharon Lerner
Nina B. Link
Jeffrey Moss
Robert Oksner
Norman Stiles
Daniel Wilcox

ILLUSTRATED BY:

Tom Cooke
A. Delaney
Larry DiFiori
Mary Grace Eubank
Michael Frith
Joe Mathieu
Michael J. Smollin
Maggie Swanson
Bob Taylor

PHOTOGRAPHS BY:

Neil Selkirk
View-Master International Group

ISBN: 0-8343-0052-4 (set); 0-8343-0054-0 (vol. 2)

Oscar Has a Bad Dream

One night Oscar the Grouch had a bad dream. In fact, he had a terrible dream.

Oscar dreamed that one morning he opened the lid of his old, banged-up trash can and it wasn't old and banged-up any more. In fact, it was all shiny and pretty and freshly painted and tied with a big red bow. Oscar was so surprised that all he could do was open his mouth, but no noise came out. He looked again at the nice white paint and the flowers painted on the outside, and opened his mouth again. Only this time, a lot of noise came out.

"I don't believe it. I just don't believe it! Somebody ruined my nice dirty, dented-up garbage can. This is awful. Look how yucchy it looks now. I am so upset I'm going to Mr.

Hooper's store and have a nice, cold anchovy ice-cream soda to cool me off."

Oscar went into Mr. Hooper's store, climbed up on the stool and said, "Hi, Mr. Hooper. I'm rotten and I hope you're the same. Give me my old favorite, an anchovy ice-cream soda. And don't expect me to say please, because grouches don't say nice things like that."

Mr. Hooper smiled at Oscar and said, "Anchovy soda? I'm sorry, but we don't have any anchovy ice cream. We only have nice-tasting ice cream, like vanilla and chocolate and strawberry."

"Wait a minute. Are you telling me that you don't have any of my favorite ice cream any more? No more spinach ice cream? No more onion ice cream? Just disgusting vanilla and chocolate? Well, never mind.

"The Mudman is coming with my weekly delivery of delicious mud. I'll just wait for him."

Oscar went back to his trash can, hiding his eyes so he couldn't see how nice it looked, and went inside. Soon there was a knock on the lid. Oscar opened it and stuck his head out. It was the Mudman.

"Boy, am I glad to see you. I can hardly wait for my nice, delicious bottles of mud."

"Mud? Excuse me, Oscar. But I'm not bringing you any mud. I'm bringing you some nice, fresh bottles of milk!"

"Milk?? Are you kidding? I don't drink milk. It's too good for you. I want my slimy old mud. That's what I want."

"But, Oscar, I wouldn't bring anybody *mud* to drink. That's

disgusting. Oh, by the way, your garbage can looks very nice."

"Ughhh!" cried Oscar. "I don't believe this is happening to me. No anchovy ice cream. No mud. My poor, wonderful, beat-up garbage can all shiny and ruined. I know what I'm gonna do. I'm gonna see my old friend Leon at the crummy dump. He'll be in his nice, broken-down shack with rags for curtains and he'll make me feel better. Yep. That's where I'm going because I can't stand it here."

Oscar began walking to the dump. He walked in the gutter, of course, because that was his favorite place to walk. Usually Oscar found old tin cans or empty soda bottles to kick, and all sorts of trash and rubbish to pick up and save.

"Hey. Wait a minute. What is going on?? I've been walking for five minutes and there's no trash in this gutter. It is clean. In fact, everything looks neat and clean. This is terrible! Boy, wait until I see my friend Leon at the dump. Something weird is going on around here."

In his dream, Oscar arrived at the dump. And he was surprised again.

"I must be seeing things!" Oscar cried. "Leon, my old grouchy friend, is all neat and dressed up! The old town dump, which used to be messy and dirty and full of busted furniture and trash, is now all neat and clean and the trash isn't trash anymore. It's fixed up and looks nice and new again! And Leon's house is fixed up and has new white curtains. This is terrible. This is yucchy! This is disgusting! Leon, what is going on??"

"Why, Oscar, I don't know what you're talking about. I wouldn't like an awful, messy, dirty dump. And I wouldn't live in a broken-down, falling-apart old shack with dirty rags for curtains. But come inside and have a nice hot plate of delicious chicken stew."

"Delicious chicken stew?? You used to make delicious garbage stew from potato peelings and eggshells with an old galosh tossed in for flavor. Chicken stew? *Yucchy!*"

Oscar didn't know what to do. His trash can was covered with flowers and fresh paint. Mr. Hooper didn't have anchovy sodas or Oscar's favorite ice cream. The Mudman had milk instead of nice, gooey mud. The gutters all over town were nice and clean. Even the town dump was all fixed up and spiffy.

"I must be going crazy," cried Oscar. "There's no trash blowing around here. Everything's so neat and clean I can't stand it! How's a grouch supposed to live in a place like this?"

Oscar's terrible dream made him toss and roll around in his sleep. Finally, he fell right out of bed and onto the floor and woke up. "Hey! I was only having a bad dream.

Whew! I was getting worried. Heh, heh! Boy, wouldn't it be terrible if everything really was all nice and neat? Thank goodness that was only a bad dream. Guess I'll go outside now and see who I can yell at."

Oscar pushed up the lid of his garbage can and almost fell out. His garbage can looked just the way it did in his dream! It was freshly painted, it had flowers all over it, and tied around it was a big red ribbon. Oscar looked around wildly. There was no trash in the gutter. The street, sidewalk and gutter were clean.

"Oh, no. I'm wide awake and it looks like I'm still dreaming! What is happening to me??"

"Why, nothing's happening to you, Oscar," Maria said to him.

"Everything is nice and clean because we're having Clean-Up Week here on Sesame Street."

"Whew!" said Oscar. "For a minute I thought I was dreaming again. Clean-Up Week, huh? Well, I'm so happy that it's not my dream coming true that I might even help."

So Oscar straightened the bow on his garbage can and went back inside.

"But don't tell anybody!" he yelled as the lid slammed shut.

Mr. Snuffle-upagus

Home:	Snuffle-cave, Sesame Street
Favorite Foods:	Spaghetti and cabbage
Best Friend:	Big Bird
Favorite Activities:	Taking naps, visiting Big Bird
Favorite Vacation:	Trip to Hawaii with Big Bird
Size:	12 feet long from the tip of his snuffle to the end of his tail
Favorite Wish:	To meet Big Bird's friends
Favorite Saying:	"Oh, dear."

Find the things that begin with the letter B.

I Used to Be Afraid

by Grover and Ernie

When I was little I used to be scared
Of being alone in the night.
I'd pull the blankets up over my head
And pray that the sky would get light...

But then my mommy sat by my bed
And said there was nothing to fear,
'Cause nothing scary went on in the night
And she and my daddy were near.

When I was little I used to be scared
Of taking a bath in the tub.
I thought when the water ran down the drain
That I would go with it...Glub-Glub.

But my old buddy Bert said,
"Come on, use your brain.
If you just take a look, you will see
That you NEVER could fit
through that very small drain!"

Now my tubby's where I love to be.

This is a great story, Ernie. It's full of words that begin with the letter B!

Bb

You know something, Bert? I'm bored.

Bert and the Beanstalk

Once upon a time, there lived a boy named Bert. One day Bert traded the family bicycle for a bag of magic beans.

But Bert's buddy, Ernie, looked in the bag and said, "Beans? Blah! How boring." And he threw the boring beans out the back window.

Immediately, the beans began to bloom. By breakfast, they had blossomed into a big, beautiful beanstalk.

When Ernie saw the beanstalk he said, "Look. A big, beautiful beanstalk. That's *really* boring."

But Bert wasn't a bit bored. "I feel brave!" Bert bellowed. So he bounded up the beanstalk.

Up, up, up went Bert, beyond the bean blossoms, beyond the birds, beyond the blue . . . until he came to a big black building.

The building belonged to a giant named Burly Barney. Burly Barney was in the bedroom eating his breakfast of bushels of buttered buns, barrels of blueberries and bunches of bananas. When Bert saw how big Burly Barney was, Bert beat it to the back room.

There, Bert found a big basket. It was full of bottlecaps.

"Boy, oh boy, oh boy!" said Bert. "Bottlecaps! I collect bottlecaps!" So Bert brought the basket of bottlecaps back to the beanstalk.

But Burly Barney saw Bert, and he began to bellow, "You took my bottlecaps!" "I'd better beat it," said Bert.

Boldly, Bert climbed down. Barney bounded down behind him. But, on a bottom branch, Bert slipped and fell with a bump.

"I'll bet you want to bash me because I borrowed your basket of bottlecaps," blurted Bert.

"Are you batty?" bellowed Burly Barney. "Those bottlecaps are boring! They were driving me bananas! Thank you for borrowing my bottlecaps!"

And Burly Barney shook Bert's hand. In fact, he shook Bert's whole body. Then Barney bounded back up the beanstalk to his beautiful black building.

And now that the basket of bottlecaps belonged to Bert, Bert had the best and biggest bunch of bottlecaps on the block. So Bert was beaming.

And everyone lived blissfully ever after. Except Ernie . . . who was bored.

Oh, brother— that's BORING!

Summer

Sing a song of summer!
Sing a song of sun!
Sing a song of swimming!
Sing a song of fun!

Sing a song of castles!
Sing a song of sand!
Sing a song of fishing!
Isn't summer grand?

COLORES   COLORS

Say it in Spanish!

azul
blue

verde
green

amarillo
yellow

violeta
purple

anaranjado
orange

rojo
red

Hello, everybodeee! Lovable Grover is here, with my new hobby—I am trying to catch this very beautiful butterfly. Look at those pretty wings! Look how gracefully she flies! What a lovely creature of nature!

On second thought, maybe I will not catch her. I will just look at her!

Nighttime

Good night.

moon

sleep

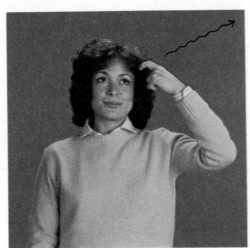

dreams

stars

yawn

How many things in this picture can you "sign"?

Good night! Have sweet dreams.

Good night!

Have

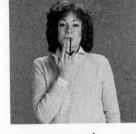
sweet

dreams.

⌘ A BIRD'S TALE ⌘

Once upon a time, a long, long time ago, there were two birds who lived together in a little cottage in the woods. The two birds were very good friends...but they didn't know what to call each other. They had no names!

One day the larger bird said to the smaller bird, "Hey! I know! I'm yellow! You can call me Yellow Bird!!"

"That's no good," replied the smaller bird. "I'm

yellow too! If we call you Yellow Bird, what will we call *me*?"

"Oh, that's true," said the large bird. "Well, how about this...I am all covered with feathers. You could call me Feathery Bird!"

"I have feathers too," said the small bird. "That's no good."

"Well, how about my feet?" said the large bird. "You could call me Orange-Feet-With-Three-Toes! How would *that* be?"

"I have orange feet with three toes also," said the small bird sadly.

"What about calling me Bird-With-Big-Googly-Eyes-and-A-Beak-Instead-Of-A-Nose-With-A-Red-Hat!" suggested the large bird.

The small bird sighed. "I have big googly eyes and I have a beak instead of a nose...and there's my red hat hanging over there on the hook."

"Oh, dear," said the large bird. "We seem to be exactly the same in every way. We'll just have to have the same name, too. There is absolutely nothing at all to tell us apart."

"Except that you're so big and I'm so little," said the small bird.

"That's it!" yelled the large bird. "I'm big and you're little!! That's the answer!! We'll call me... Great Huge Enormous Bird...and we'll call you... Wee Tiny Small Bird!"

"How's about just Big Bird and Little Bird, huh?"

With Love from Me to Me

Hello, everybody! Let us play a little word game. Here is a picture of me, cute little Grover. Do you see the lines pointing to parts of my furry body? You do? Oh, good. Near each line is a word. Do you know what the words say? Guess. The word that is matched to my leg says ___. Yes! That is right! It says LEG. Guess what the other words say.

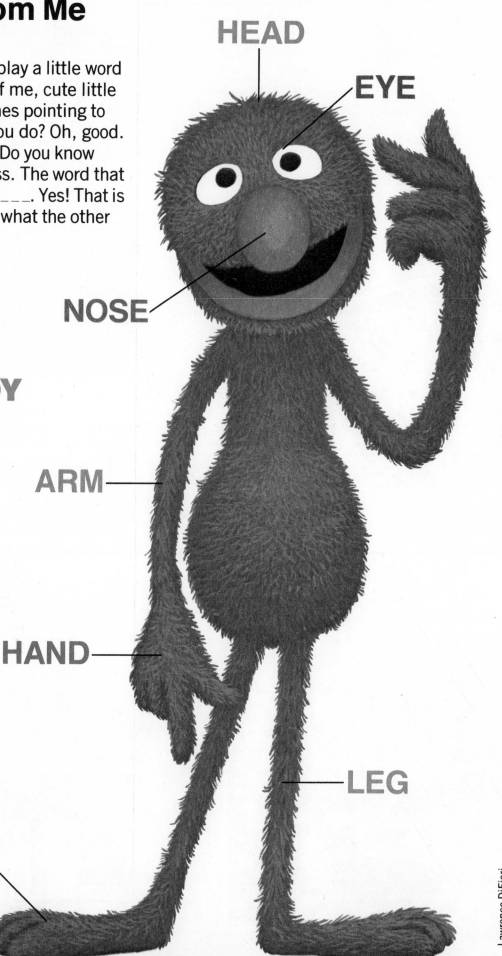

HEAD

EYE

NOSE

BODY

ARM

HAND

LEG

FOOT

Now I will tell you a story. All those nice words are in this story. Will you help me? See if you can tell what all the words in pretty colors say. Here we go!

Foot, I like you, Foot.

One day, I said **FOOT**, I like you, **FOOT**. You can hop. **LEG**, I said, I like you, **LEG**. You are a friend of **FOOT**. **HAND**, I said, I like you. You are fun. **ARM**, I said, you are wonderful, **ARM**. You can lift my **HAND** way up. **EYE**, I said, I am so proud that you can see things. **NOSE**, I said, I love you, **NOSE**. You are so cute. **HEAD**, I said, Grover likes you very much. You are always thinking.

So, I made my **FOOT**, **LEG**, **HAND**, **ARM**, **EYE**, **NOSE** and **HEAD** feel very good that day. The end.

A Very Old Shape Story

One day, a very long time ago, a cave man was pulling a box of rocks. "This rock box is so hard to pull," the cave man complained, "that by the time I get to my rock garden I'm too tired to do anything."

Then the cave man had a terrific idea. "I'll put some things under the rock box to make it roll," he shouted out.

He went to his cave. Since triangles were his favorite shape, he decided to use triangles. After many hours of hard work, the cave man had hammered out four stone triangles. He attached them to his rock box and began to pull. Because the triangles had three corners, they couldn't roll.

He pulled
and pulled...

until...

the rope broke.

"I really do love triangles, but maybe I'd better use squares instead," he thought to himself. So he went back to the cave and hammered out four stone squares.

He attached them to his rock box and pulled. The squares were even harder to pull than the triangles because they had four corners. Again the rope broke.

"I guess this wasn't such a hot idea," the cave man mumbled as he kicked a big round rock sitting in his path. The round rock began to roll down the hill.

"Round!" the cave man yelled. "Why didn't I think of that before?"

So he hurried home and hammered out four round stones. When he attached them to his rock box the round stones rolled smoothly along because they didn't have any corners.

Pretty soon all his neighbors wanted round stones for their rock boxes, too, so the cave man opened up a Round Stone Shop in his cave. "I think I'll call these round stones...*bananas*," the cave man announced—and so he did.

The End

Big Bird's Banana Bread

Let's make banana bread!
It's better than
a birdseed sundae!
It's easy.
Just follow the directions.

Here is what you will need:
3 peeled ripe bananas
3/4 cup honey
1/4 cup melted butter
1/2 teaspoon baking soda
1 1/2 cups whole wheat flour
1 big bowl
1 big wooden spoon
1 fork
1 bread pan (rub some cooking oil around the inside of it)
1 wire cooling rack
1 measuring cup
1 set of measuring spoons

Here's what you need a grownup to do:
1. Turn the oven on to 350 degrees.
2. Melt 1/4 cup of butter in a pan.
I asked Mr. Looper to help me.
He was happy to help!

Here's what you do:

1 Put the peeled bananas in a bowl.

2 Mash up the bananas with the back of a fork.

3 Add the melted butter.

4 Add:
1/2 teaspoon baking soda
1 1/2 cups whole wheat flour
3/4 cup honey

5 Stir everything in the bowl with the big spoon. Stir until everything is mixed together.

6 Pour the mix into the oiled bread pan.

7 Bake for one hour.

8 After one hour, put a toothpick in the bread.
Is there some bread on the toothpick when you pull it out?
If there is, let the bread cook for a little while longer.
If there is no bread on the toothpick when you pull it out, the bread is done!

9 Ask your grown-up helper to take the bread out of the oven.
They need to take the bread out of the pan, and put it on the wire rack.

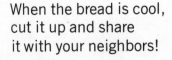

10 When the bread is cool, cut it up and share it with your neighbors!

The Count's Counting Page

Upside down! Upside down!
I am counting upside down.
This is what I love to do
When I count up to 2.

2 nice dragons! 2 sly elves!
2 small castles on the shelves!
2 big spiders! 2 plum pies!
All these 2's before my eyes!

2 big moons, 2 piles of gold!
2 mean witches—very old.
2 bright stars shine on the town!
All these 2's are upside down!

Upside down! Upside down!
I am counting upside down!
This is what I love to do
When I count up to 2.

Turn this picture right side up.
Find the things that come in 2's.

Sherlock Hemlock
in
"The Mysterious Stranger"

THE CAT AND THE FIDDLE

Hey, diddle, diddle!
The cat and the fiddle,
  The cow jumped over the moon;
The little dog laughed
To see such sport,
  And the dish ran away with the spoon.